All Around Me I See

By Laya Steinberg

Illustrated by Cris Arbo

Dawn Publications

To my parents Victor and Shirley
for their unending love and support. – LS

For the wonderful girls in my family:
Ari, Julie, Lina, Lisi, Sarah, and a special thank you to Makayla. – CA

Copyright © 2005 Laya Steinberg
Illustration copyright © 2005 Cris Arbo

A SHARING NATURE WITH CHILDREN BOOK

Library of Congress Cataloging-in-Publication Data

Steinberg, Laya.
  All around me, I see / by Laya Steinberg ; illustrated by Cris Arbo.-- 1st
ed.
      p. cm. -- (A sharing nature with children book)
  Summary: Illustrations and simple, rhyming text detail what a young girl
observes during her first camping trip--even while she is dreaming.
  ISBN 1-58469-068-2 (hardback) -- ISBN 1-58469-069-0 (pbk.)
  [1. Nature--Fiction. 2. Dreams--Fiction. 3. Stories in rhyme.] I. Arbo,
Cris, ill. II. Title. III. Series.
  PZ8.3.S8195Al 2005
  [E]--dc22
                          2004018936

Dawn Publications
12402 Bitney Springs Road
Nevada City, CA 95959
530-274-7775
nature@dawnpub.com

Manufactured by Regent Publishing Services, Hong Kong
Printed November 2009 in ShenZhen, Guangdong, China

10 9 8 7 6 5 4 3 2
First Edition

Design and computer production by Patty Arnold, Menagerie Design and Publishing

The rain is a drink for the Earth.

A puddle is a bath for a bird.

A stream is a path to the ocean.

A whale sings a song to be heard.

A turtle makes a bridge from a log.

The grass is a bed for a deer.

A blossom is a bowl for dew.

A nest is a cradle for eggs.

A branch is an owl's point of view.

The sun is like warmth from a fire.

The sky is a place to be free.

The moon is a light in the darkness.

This Earth is a home for me.

Photo courtesy of Betsy Bassett

As the founder and a teacher in the outdoor classroom and organic garden at the Burr Elementary School in Auburndale, Massachusetts, Laya Steinberg sees how surprised and excited children are to discover the unfolding mysteries at their feet. In writing this book, Laya set out to show the connections and beauty of nature through simple analogies.

A native of Martha's Vineyard Island, Cris Arbo received her degree in art and theater from William Paterson University. Her art has appeared in books, magazines, calendars, cards, murals, and in animated feature films, TV shows, and commercials. When not at the drawing board, she gardens and explores the beautiful countryside near her home in rural central Virginia. She and her husband, author Joseph Patrick Anthony, are frequent speakers at schools and conventions. This is the third book she has illustrated for Dawn Publications.

OTHER BOOKS ILLUSTRATED BY CRIS ARBO

The Dandelion Seed and *In A Nutshell* by Joseph Anthony. Both the world travels of a wind-blown dandelion seed and the life story of an acorn are simple, uplifting tales with profound underlying metaphors for life.

A FEW OTHER NATURE AWARENESS TITLES FROM THE DAWN PUBLICATIONS

Stickeen: John Muir and the Brave Little Dog by Donnell Rubay. This classic true story of John Muir's favorite wilderness adventure transformed the relationship between Muir and a dog.

Eliza and the Dragonfly by Susie Caldwell Rinehart. Almost despite herself, Eliza becomes entranced by the "awful" dragonfly nymph—and before long, both of them are transformed.

Over in the Ocean: In a Coral Reef and *Over in the Jungle: a Rainforest Rhyme* by Marianne Berkes, illustrated by Jeanette Canyon. Stunning clay art accompanies delightful lyrics based on the classic tune of "Over in the Meadow."

Sunshine On My Shoulders, Ancient Rhymes: A Dolphin Lullaby, Take Me Home Country Roads, Grandma's Feather Bed and *For Baby (For Bobbie)* by John Denver make his most child-friendly and nature-aware lyrics a delightful new experience. The hardback version comes with a CD of John singing the song.

Dawn Publications is dedicated to inspiring in children a deeper understanding and appreciation for all life on Earth. Call 800-545-7475 or visit us online at www.dawnpub.com.